The Dark Cloud Series
FINDS TREES

Written and Illustrated
By Brittany Cummings

Dedicated to my amazing son, Dominic.

I love you with all my heart

Once upon a time, there was a big, dark cloud. He was very full of rain and needed to give the trees a drink of water. But he didn't know what trees looked like, so he set off to ask someone.

The dark cloud saw a helicopter flying quickly towards him.

"Mr. Helicopter, what do trees look like?"

The helicopter did not stop and went zooming by the dark cloud. So, he went to find someone else to ask.

He noticed a duck swimming in the pond below and floated down to him.

"Mr. Duck, what do trees look like?"

"Quack!" said the duck.

"What does that mean?" replied the dark cloud.

"Quack!"

So the dark cloud went to find someone else to ask and spotted a cow in the meadow.

"Mr. Cow, what do trees look like?"

The cow said, "Moo!"

"What does that mean?" replied the dark cloud.

"Moo!"

So the dark cloud went to find someone else to ask and saw a little boy sitting on a swing.

"Little boy, what do trees look like?"

The little boy laughed and said, "Silly dark cloud. The trees are all around you. They have brown trunks and green leaves on the top."

The dark cloud looked all around him and saw all the trees! He was so excited!

"Oh thank you, little boy!" and he went way up high, back into the sky, and started raining, giving all the trees a drink of water.

About Brittany Cummings

My name is Brittany. Born and raised in East Tennessee. I'm a Jesus-follower, family loving, football and hockey fan.

I worked as a veterinary technician while I finished my psychology and English degrees from the University of Tennessee. I then worked as a counselor for children with mental health issues. Now, I have the best "job" in the world: stay-at-home-mom.

My story telling began with stories for my son's bedtime. My husband encouraged me to get my stories published, and so my journey began.

We are blessed with an extraordinary son, three dogs, and a fish. We have an amazing extended family who love and care for us dearly.

My hobbies include baking with my son, scrapbooking, reading, watching movies, and going on family walks.

God has given me so much, and I'm excited to see what other plans He has for me.

Cover and Illustrations: Brittany Cummings

Cover and Illustrations copyright © 2020 Brittany Cummings & Seventh Star Press, LLC.

Editor: Holly Phillippe

Published by Seventh StarChild

ISBN: 978-1-7362781-7-8

Seventh StarChild is an imprint of Seventh Star Press

www.seventhstarpress.com

info@seventhstarpress.com

Publisher's Note:

Finds Trees is a work of fiction. All names, characters, and places are the product of the author's imagination, used in fictitious manner. Any resemblances to actual persons, places, locales, events, etc. are purely coincidental.

Printed in the United States of America

First Edition

CPSIA information can be obtained at www.ICGtesting.com
Printed in the USA
BVIW122311030221
599226BV00018B/151